Move Over, ROVER!

Karen Beaumont

Illustrated by
Jane Dyer

Harcourt, Inc.

Orlando Austin New York San Diego Toronto London

Manufactured in China

Rover's in the doghouse,
chewing on a bone.
What a day to romp and play!
Too bad he's all alone.

Oh, my, look at the sky!
Thunder! Lightning!
Mighty frightening!

Rain is pouring....
Oh, how boring.

Rover's in the doghouse,
sleeping through the storm....
Cat is looking all around
to find a place that's warm.

Move over, Rover!

Cat's in the doghouse,
sleeping through the storm....
Raccoon is looking all around
to find a place that's warm.

Skit-scat, Cat!
Move over, Rover!

Raccoon's in the doghouse,
sleeping through the storm....
Squirrel is looking all around
to find a place that's warm.

Make room, Raccoon!
Skit-scat, Cat!
Move over, Rover!

Squirrel's in the doghouse,
sleeping through the storm. . . .
Blue Jay's looking all around
to find a place that's warm.

Squeeze in, Squirrel!
Make room, Raccoon!
Skit-scat, Cat!
Move over, Rover!

Blue Jay's in the doghouse,
sleeping through the storm....
Snake is looking all around
to find a place that's warm.

Out of the way, Blue Jay!
Squeeze in, Squirrel!
Make room, Raccoon!
Skit-scat, Cat!
Move over, Rover!

Snake's in the doghouse,
sleeping through the storm....
Mouse is looking all around
to find a place that's warm.

Slide aside, Snake!
Out of the way, Blue Jay!
Squeeze in, Squirrel!
Make room, Raccoon!
Skit-scat, Cat!
Move over, Rover!

Tight fit. Might split.
Sorry, Mouse. Full house!

Crowded in the doghouse,
all are sleeping well.
But then...sniff, sniff!
They catch a whiff!
What's that awful smell?

Skitter, scatter!
What's the matter?
Scamper, scurry!
What's the hurry?

Skunk's in the doghouse,
sleeping through the storm....
The rest are racing round to find
another place that's warm.

Oh, my, look at the sky!
Storm's over.
Where's Rover?

Romping?   Racing?

Jumping?

Chasing?

No!

Rover's in the doghouse,
chewing on a bone.
Soaked and sopping,
tail flip-flopping,
happy he's alone!

For my Uncle Bill,
with love and gratitude
—K. B.

For Woolly
—J. D.

Text copyright © 2006 by Karen Beaumont
Illustrations copyright © 2006 by Jane Dyer

www.HarcourtBooks.com

Library of Congress Cataloging-in-Publication Data
Beaumont, Karen.
Move over, Rover!/Karen Beaumont; [illustrated by] Jane Dyer.
p. cm.
Summary: When a storm comes, Rover expects to have his doghouse all to himself
but finds that various other animals, including a skunk, come to join him.
[1. Dogs—Fiction.   2. Animals—Fiction.   3. Stories in rhyme.]
I. Dyer, Jane, ill. II. Title.
PZ8.3.B3845Mov 2006
[E]—dc22   2005014557
ISBN-13: 978-0-15-201979-2   ISBN-10: 0-15-201979-0

H G F E D C B

The illustrations in this book were done in watercolor and liquid acrylic
on Arches 140 lb. hot press watercolor paper.
The display type was hand lettered by Judythe Sieck.
The text type was set in Memphis.
Color separations by Colourscan Co. Pte. Ltd., Singapore
Manufactured by SNP Leefung Holdings Limited, China
This book was printed on totally chlorine-free Stora Enso Matte paper.
Production supervision by Ginger Boyer
Designed by Lauren Rille